# Can I Sit with You?

**Sarah Jacoby**

chronicle books · san francisco

Library of Congress Cataloging-in-Publication Data:

Names: Jacoby, Sarah (Illustrator), author, illustrator.

Title: Can I sit with you? / Sarah Jacoby.

Description: San Francisco : Chronicle Books, 2021. | Audience: Ages 5-8. | Audience: Grades K-1. | Summary: A scruffy stray dog follows a girl home, promising to stay by her side and be her loyal friend and companion for as long as she needs.

Identifiers: LCCN 2019043467 | ISBN 9781452164649 (hardcover)

Subjects: LCSH: Dogs—Juvenile fiction. | Human-animal relationships—Juvenile fiction. | Friendship—Juvenile fiction. | Stories in rhyme. | CYAC: Stories in rhyme. | Dogs—Fiction. | Human-animal relationships—Fiction. | Friendship—Fiction. | LCGFT: Stories in rhyme. | Picture books.

Classification: LCC PZ8.3.J14 Can 2020 | DDC [E]—dc23

LC record available at https://lccn.loc.gov/2019043467

Manufactured in China.

Design by Amelia Mack.

Typeset in Monod Brun.

The illustrations in this book were rendered in watercolor, NuPastel, and mixed media.

10 9 8 7 6 5 4 3 2 1

Chronicle Books LLC

680 Second Street

San Francisco, California 94107

Chronicle Books—we see things differently. Become part of our community at www.chroniclekids.com.

to Walt, Wheez, Butchie & Lil Pajamas

Pardon me—

May I ask you a question?

If you are brimming
like a ringing bell,

if you are lonely
like an empty plate,

if you are dusty eyed,              if you are bright—

Can I sit with you?

If you take a long car ride          or find a different chair,

if the day is strange and new

I'll be familiar, loyal, true.

When you want a wide green field,

when you want the orange light,

when you need a deep blue dark—

Can I sit with you?

Back and forth, to and fro,
we weave the space between.

Bit by bit, throw by throw,
we start to feel at ease.

So if you hear another call
or disappear from view,

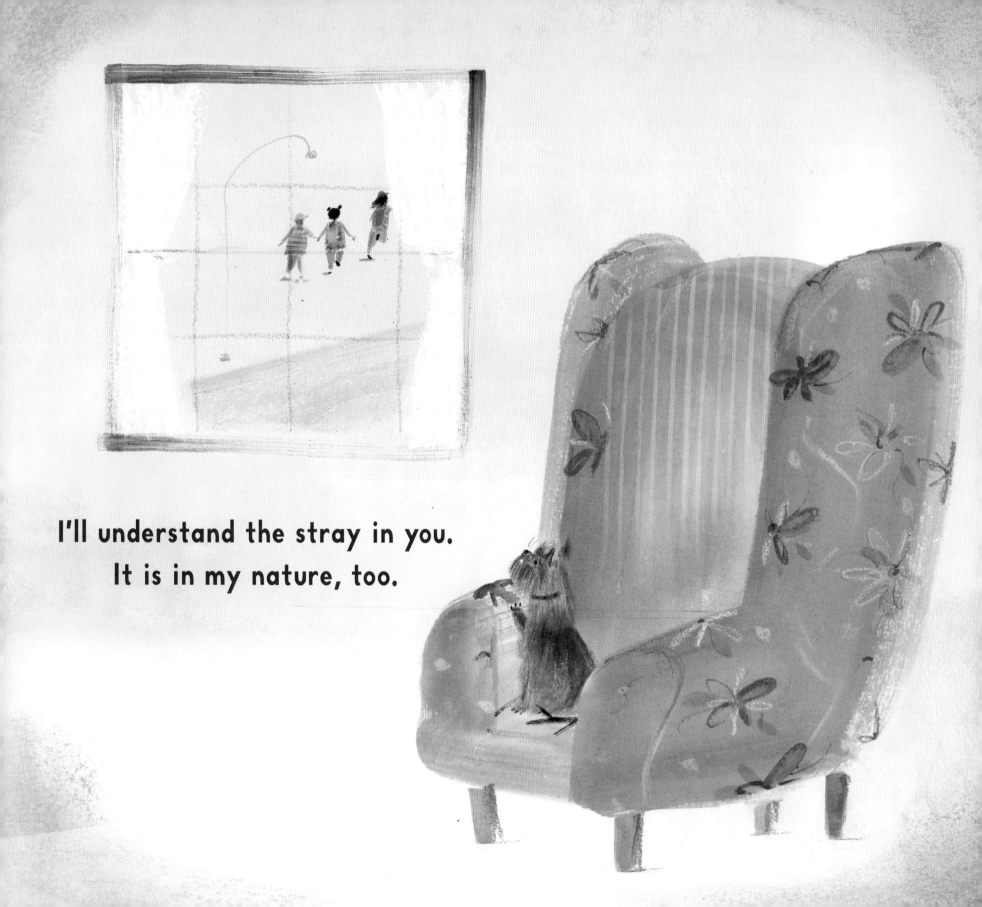

I'll understand the stray in you.
It is in my nature, too.

And even if you wander,
ramble, and roam,

I know looking high and low

can show you what you left at home.

I've wandered many ways
    and I've seen so much new.
I've felt many colors,
    still I recall our blue.
Now I hear this echo
    I'm singing back to you,

a long awaited answer—

I will sit with you.